1001
Words

University of Talk
Volume Five

Editor:
Ian Clayton

Art Circus Education
1996

Published by **Yorkshire Art Circus**, School Lane, Glasshoughton, Castleford, West Yorkshire, WF10 4QH

© Stories: Yorkshire Art Circus and contributing authors
© Illustrations: Alan Davis, Les Plumb, Harry Malkin
© Cover Design: Paul Miller
Production: John Armitstead, Fiona Blair, Ian Daley, Ziya Dikbas
Guy Goodair, Lorna Hey, David Jennings

Printed by Peepal Tree Press, Leeds

ISBN: 1 898311 31 5

ACE *Talking Into Books* tutor: Ian Clayton

Art Circus Education (ACE) is arts based practical training in an informal workplace atmosphere. It combines traditional skills like storytelling, writing and craft techniques with new technology and works towards an end product. This book is the result. ACE is the education wing of Yorkshire Art Circus.

ACE runs an annual programme of workshops in writing, visual arts, computers, publishing and performance. For details of current courses ring 01977 550401 and ask for Ian Daley or Lorna Hey.

Art Circus Education is supported by:

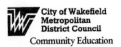

Contents

Introduction

The Art Circus Education *Talking into Books* class has been running every Thursday morning for the last seven years. In that time the different groups who have come and gone have produced very varied books; stories from the pits, licorice factories, stories about unemployment and more recently a collection of ghost stories. The class of 1995/96 were challenged to write a short story about relationships in no more than 1001 words. I haven't counted every word in every story so I hope nobody has cheated.

The stories vary in subject matter and style. At Art Circus Education we believe quality comes at all levels of involvement. The writers you will read here are beginner writers, they will I'm sure come on leaps and bounds, if the way they have approached this first stepping stone into print is anything to go by.

Ian Clayton

Too Close For Comfort

John Turner

As I turned off the A62, deeper into brass band territory, I felt guilty. I should have made the effort to visit Jack and Sheila Robinson ages ago. Their only child Alice had been my first love and she promised to wait for me and they were old family friends. They had seemed elderly when I last saw them, so they must be ancient by now. I reckoned it was pretty brave of them to be asking me to stay.

I stopped near the museum to get my bearings. It had been nearly ten years since I had last seen Alice. As I moved out from the village and under the bridge the memories came flooding back. It was there Alice and me did our courting. A smile passed over my face, she said she would wait for me, - " turn right, up the hill and first right down an unmarked lane just past the turn to South Diggle. The cottage is on the right on the second bad bend. It's got red gates."

It was dark when I found the cottage. The gates were broken and in deep neglect. I sat in the car for a moment, and heard a dog barking. Then I took the plunge.

Jack and Sheila welcomed me like a long-lost son. After all I had nearly married their daughter. It wasn't until they sat me down at the kitchen table with a glass of gooseberry wine that I had a chance to look at them properly. God they were even more doddering than when I had known them all those years ago. Jack had cut himself shaving and had a big blob of cotton-wool on his chin. His glasses were held together with sticking plaster. There were stains down his pullover. He wore no socks and had tatty boots with the laces trailing. Sheila, who was stirring something on the stove, seemed to be wearing old velvet curtains tied round the middle with one of Jack's ties. She walked badly, clutching the edges of tables and chairs. The kitchen was filthy. A baldish dog in the corner scratched and scratched. On the old Welsh dresser stood a gleamingly polished trumpet. The only clean thing in the place.

"Sheila falls over sometimes," Jack told me proudly, as he watched her laboriously stoop to pick up the wooden spoon she had dropped and plunge it back in her saucepan. "Her knees are going. And her hips. And she can't see a thing."

"And you leave the gas on. And once you went out without your trousers." She cackled with pleasure at the memory.

"Alice wants to put us into a home," Jack went on, and they both fell about laughing. Sheila turned from her saucepan to glance at Jack admiringly. "But we're not going to go," she said. "Did I tell you we're having a tiny dinner party tonight? Just like old times."

"Is Alice coming?" I asked. "Can I help in any way?"

"Jack, show John his room," commanded Sheila. Clearly she didn't want any help.

My room was icy. There was a radiator, but it was cold. The wallpaper was peeling off with black mould showing beneath. Judging from the limp dampness of the sheets, the bed had been made up several years ago.

I had planned to change for dinner, but couldn't bear even to take my sweater off. The Robinson's were not only earnestly old and earnestly dirty, they were probably earnestly poor too. I'd brought them two bottles of Australian wine. Perhaps I should have brought cakes and chocolate as well. But then I remembered Alice and how she used to be all those years ago.

Downstairs, there was a loud female voice and barks from the dog. Alice had arrived.

Alice, who I hadn't seen for many years, had put on weight. But I could still see why I'd always fancied her. There she was in a two-piece, a bulging overnight bag in her hand. We exchanged the kind of rapturous, nostalgic embrace that the situation demanded. But I felt she was put out by my presence. I couldn't think why. She went upstairs to her room and thumped about; I guessed she had her own sheets in that bag.

We ate early, soon after seven. The dinner was unspeakable. The soup was thin with misshapen croutons floating in it. The croutons were that dry food which you sprinkle from a packet for dogs, I'm sure. I was given the job of cutting the bread. The main course was a meat stew cooked to a pulp, with grisly bits in. When I got up to help Sheila clear the plates, I saw through the open pantry door that there was nothing at all on the shelves except tins of dog food. Jack and Sheila drank the wine. Alice stuck to gin which she had brought with her.

Her parents grew more and more mellow on the wine. They beamed at each other and at us. They told incomprehensible jokes and reminisced about the past.

"Did I tell you of that time she had to go to the jumble sale to get our Alice a pair of knickers before she could go to school?" Jack laughed uncontrollably as he fixed his stare in my direction.

"Ay, and you had to pawn your trumpet to get the money. And nowt much's changed," Sheila retorted mercilessly.

Alice sat with a fixed smile. She kept looking at her watch.

"Alice, remember how we used to hold hands under the bridge. You said you would wait for me."

"Yes, yes I did. That was a long time ago John. I waited..."

Her voice trailed to nothing. She glanced to the dresser and just stared. It was a picture of Alice holding hands with a stocky middle aged man. Two children stood in front of them. He was older than me. Looked like me. But it wasn't me... A very close shave indeed.

Hello Mr Malbis

Elsie Sykes

'This is definitely the last time Nina Barry' I promised myself, as I listened outside the bedroom door. It was a distasteful habit, sneaky and juvenile, but one I found impossible to break whilst the children kept coming.

When the little body turned in the bed, rustling the covers, heaving a shaky sigh, I waited, tight and still, so every sound could percolate through.

"Hello Mr Malbis." I heard him say. "Are you my friend?"

I moved quickly then, covering my mouth, pressing myself hard against the wall. Expelling my breath, slow and quiet. So difficult, now the familiar swelling in my chest was back. That ache when I needed to cry. Tears for him. Tears for me and tears for all the others.

When you foster, 'No experience is ever wasted', and I was glad I had remembered. It was the moon reminded me. That full moon of my childhood, hanging bright over the rooftops when I turned down the child's bed. It had stayed, my hand on the curtains, melting the years until the phone rang.

"It's okay Sam! I'll get it!" I called, making my voice casual hoping he would stay with the TV. But I was too late. He was across the hall like lightening, turning my effort down the stairs into slow motion replay.

"Is that my daddy?" he asked. His eager five year old fingers handling the receiver like it was a dumb bell. Scoring over my leaden feet after three months of this game with the phone.

I stood, helpless, while he whispered. "No. There's no mummy here. Only Aunty Neen," and my heart sank, matching the dejected slope of his shoulders.

"Someone for me?" I asked, forcing a brightness that refused to polish the steel growing between my ribs as he surrendered the phone.

"Hello? Yes. Speaking," and brushing my hand over the white blonde head, hugged the unresponsive body to my side before he slid back to the TV. "I see. Right." The voice on the phone droned the usual excuses whilst my lips tightened over words, millions of words I wanted to say.

"Change of heart," the go-between was saying. Each word turning me icy cool. Controlled.

"We'll try again at the weekend then." I said. Waiting for the distant click to set me free.

Change of heart I muttered at that piece of mechanism that was ruling my life. What bloody heart? Doesn't want his son visiting prison? Self-centred, good-for-nothing. One more empty weekend I promised, banging my venom out on the phone. And I'll be saying it all.

There seemed to be no end to them, children with nobody. This one had a mother in psychiatric care and a father who had left him. Dumped him with a stranger he had to call Aunty Neen, so he could belong.

"Fish fingers alright?" I asked, watching the child's back. Eventually, the little head bobbed and that was enough. I understood. He was keeping his pain hidden in the cartoons on the screen.

We ate together, Sam doing exactly what was expected with never a smile or a tear, more lethargic than sullen. His spirit, dying by inches every time the phone rang and growing so withdrawn, it was worrying. His daddy was becoming a phantom he tucked away somewhere, for the phone or maybe bedtime.

Bathtime was strained and I prayed the clear night and the moon would stay. Grandpa's moon, nudging my memory. It was a vain hope. A tiny glimmer.

"Did you ever see so many stars Sam?" I gambled. "There's big ones and small ones!" The little head turned a fraction on the pillow. "And of course there's my friend, Mr Malbis!"

His eyes drifted towards the window and I wished.

"When I was a little girl, not much bigger than you, my mummy went away to hospital and I didn't see her for a long, long time. Then, one evening Grandpa took me in the car to see her. I was silly and got so worried, so scared, I was nearly sick."

A thumb strayed between his lips and struggling for the right words, I hitched the curtains wider, for confidence, as much as the view. I recognised his fear, his rejection. I'd watched it grow.

I leaned across the bed, close enough for touching, tucked him in and continued.

"When we passed lots of houses, all lit up, Grandpa said, "Everything will be alright now Neen. See. There's 'Acaster Malbis'. I never saw the road sign Sam. All I saw, high above the houses, was the moon."

The boy looked puzzled and feeling desperate, I nodded towards the window. This was so hard, making sense of a childish memory. Maybe I'd better leave it. Then the little head moved me aside. I was blocking the sky.

"He looked so nice, I told Mr Malbis everything. About forgetting what Mummy looked like and what if I said hello to the wrong lady. And you know what? Everything felt right again and I wasn't sick anymore."

Sliding Teddy along the pillow made kissing the cheek easy. But I musn't hug. Not yet. He wasn't ready.

"Mr Malbis is still out there you know. See. All big and shiny!"

"That's the moon Aunty Neen!" he scoffed, his tone saying idiot.

"I know! But can't you see? Those two kind eyes and that big smiley mouth. That's Mr Malbis. Mr Acaster Malbis!"

He didn't notice me leaving. His eyes were on the window.

Turning out the light, left the moon painting shadows on the wall and I wanted so much then to hold him. But he wasn't mine to hold and that was my need, not his. Foster loving at the wrong time, only hurts.

His back was turned as I closed the door, leaving me, as always, outside. Holding my breath. Listening. Then the words came. Slow and hesitant.

"Hello Mr Malbis. Are you my friend?"

The Bottle

Katie Harris

You're gone. All I see now are pictures in my head, snapshots of a relationship destined to fail. My alcoholic love. Where are you? You went away, told me you needed some space. I remember the day you left.

A fire glowing orange over coal. The mouldy smell of waste bin, old rug needing a shake. The Bottle. Hanging from a piece of string on the wall, in this kitchen, like Autumn; fading and dying. But you were there, sitting back, looking at me waiting to say something. Your eyes asked me questions. Pale green. When you're drinking they turn blue like cornflowers. How many times had we sat here, at the round pine table drinking tea from chipped *Dad* mugs, chatting about nothing above the painful screech of the baby? Now there was something to say we couldn't talk.

"Do you wish you'd never met me?" You looked intense, a rare moment.

"Yeah, I do actually."

"Why?" You asked. Your eyes focused on my face and mine focused on the wall. The Bottle on the wall.

"Because if I hadn't met you I wouldn't be so fucked up would I?"

"So you're depressed 'cause of me?" Your face was healthy now, open, with thick eyebrows furrowed, a fist on your chin and a finger filling the gap in your teeth. You had your legs crossed and the other hand was tapping the table.

"The mad thing is you make me happy. But sometimes you make me so angry I want to kill you." I got up. The baby was at the door, demanding to get out. I gave her freedom. Peace.

"Why don't you kill me then, if I make you so mad?" You said. A stupid question. I didn't answer. Quite often I think you're stupid the things you say, the way I have to explain. You turned in your seat to put a tape in the machine. I love your hair. It curls at the nape of your neck. That's why I don't kill you.

We sat waiting, looking at each other.

A car pulled up outside. I swallowed. You got up. Your eyes escaped me, focused now on the door and the bags that were huddled beside it. You pulled up your jeans and opened the front door. The wind made the hall door slam. The Bottle hung on the string and hit the wall. Nearly smashed. It came back now. I had the Bottle in my hand. Threw it to the floor. The sound of smashing glass, I'm out of control. There's fizz at my feet, liquid everywhere, on your green hiking boots. Your face is swollen, eyes empty in disbelief. Rage subsides, tears now. Your strong male face bows, pitiful with emotion, eyes shining and salty. You walk towards me, hold me too tight and can hardly stand.

"I hope you have a brilliant time." I didn't mean it. I wanted you to miss me. You kissed me goodbye in the kitchen. No hug, a short, distracted kiss. The kind you know I hate.

I waved.

A week without you. I'd cope. Stones on ropes pulling at my insides. I walked from your door, feet kicking up gravel, holding her small sticky hand. I look back and remember. You're there chopping wood in the yard, in the snow, with your stripy hat on. You're sitting on the doorstep now, tying the laces of your green hiking boots, smiling. You look up. Don't change. You're staggering towards me, eyes like cornflowers, face puffed like popcorn, a chuckle I want to kick from your mouth. I feel violent. Sick. You come closer and I can smell boredom. Drink. I look away in disgust.

You're gone.

Two days and the cloud of gloom which had plagued me for months lifted. I felt like summer, filled with sunshine. Small things made me happy; morning light on dewy grass. The baby's look of delight as I showed her cows in a field.

I needed time away from you, to think, to resolve.

The supermarket lights were crude. Orange squash. You have those lights in your kitchen. I know you're in when the window is a fluorescent rectangle.

I was pushing down the aisles, choosing things I didn't need. You're there, standing beside me, picking out yoghurt bargains, filling your basket.

"Kiss me" I whisper. You touch my chin. Fingers are gentle, you forget friends. Lips meet. My body's hot, cheeks burning.

"You've got a cherry on." I hide my face.

"We've never kissed in the supermarket." You're gone.

I was excited, nervous. Anticipating tanned body and stories of cycling through mountains in sunshine. I kept passing your door. Looking. I put a heart shaped note through the letter box.

"Come and see me when you get back. Wake me up."

You didn't come that night. I slept and woke with the empty bed. You must have been too tired. Dared not to think of possibilities. I got up, opened the curtains and showed the baby the sky, the wild garden full of brambles and tulips. You love to walk in this weather pointing out birds in their nests, eyes wide in naive surprise.

I approached your house, opened the letter box, looked. Shouted. No answer. The kitchen was empty. The letter box framed the space on the wall. The Bottle was gone. I gulped. I stuck my face against the frosted glass of the back door. Were you in the room? Disappointment. I kept looking. Dread. I can almost see you lying on the sofa with your stripy hat on. Smells of greasy hair. You are snoring, long dark stubble on your face, body covered with the cream rug. Crushed empty cans surround you. Wait. There's broken glass on the floor at your feet. Your eyes open, won't focus but you know it's me. You turn your head away.

"The Bottle's broken," you mumble.

You're gone.

My pain lifts, I'm resolved. If you come back, I'll tell you. I can't cope anymore.

YORKSHIRE AMBITION

Alice Hepworth

"Will you go over and see grandad George this morning Gary?" Sadie clattered around the kitchen putting away the breakfast things.

"Aw, mum..." Gary complained as he stuffed the last piece of toast in his mouth.

"I know... but he'll be expecting me at teatime and I can't make it." Sadie glanced across the table at Kevin, her husband, hidden behind a newspaper.

"Do I have to? I know it's holiday but exams start in three weeks and I've some swotting to do." Gary muttered, as he pushed his chair away from the table. "And this afternoon I'm going up to the cricket club. There's a match on. I told you." He tipped the crockery into the sink with a clatter.

Kevin jumped to his feet snapping the air with his newspaper. "Watch it! At this rate we'll have no pots left." He glared at his son, his mouth held in a thin line. "You should concentrate on your exams, never mind cricket." He folded his newspaper deliberately and strode to the front door shouting, "Come on, Sadie if you want a lift. I've got to be in Leeds by half-past ten."

Sadie sighed. "Yes, yes. Just let me mop the table. You get the car out and and I'll follow you." She listened for the front door banging and then, putting her arm around Gary's shoulder, she said reproachfully, "You should know better than to mention the cricket club. You know what he's like."

Gary shrugged away the enfolding arm and muttered, "Just because he was God's gift to rugby league doesn't mean I've got to like it. I'm no good at rugby, but cricket's different. He doesn't understand." Gary ran the water in the sink with a swoosh, spraying water half way up the wall. With a sigh, he turned to his mum. "I don't want to miss any matches 'cos they said last season that if I shaped up I might get a trial at Headingley. I can't let the chance slip, you know that, mum."

"Yes, I understand. But listen, you could do a couple of hours revision, then go and see grandad George. Don't be mean, Gary. He'll give you some dinner. Why don't you take him to the cricket club. He was captain for years, you know."

"I know. You've told me often enough. Hey, that might not be a bad idea. If I trot him along it'll remind the coach that cricket's in my blood. He was a mate of grandad's wasn't he?"

"You young monkey!" Sadie pretended to cuff him and he dodged her, defending himself with the teatowel. "Going to the cricket club would make his day. Mind you tell him I'll definitely see him tomorrow." Sadie pulled on her jacket and went out to the car.

"It's only me grandad. Ay-up, that smells good. I'm starving." Gary poked his head round the kitchen door to see his grandfather at the stove, stirring a pan.

"Now then lad, I've never seen you when you weren't starving. You must have holler legs. Well, there's enough here for two. Mutton stew. Your gran would've been proud of me the way I can rustle up stews."

"I'll set the table then, shall I?" Gary reached into the dresser draw and drew out a blue checked cloth. The two worked in companiable silence as the cooking was completed and the table was laid.

"Grandad, there's a match at the cricket club this aft. I'm batting at number four. Would you like to come?"

"Ee lad, I would that. I was just thinking this morning I've survived for another cricket season. Not that England's much cop just now. Yorkshire's County fixture card came this week, but I told Fred Sutton I'm in two minds as to whether I'll renew my membership. And if I don't, he won't either." George smiled at Gary, rubbing his eyes, red-rimmed and watery with what he would say was old age, but tears of pride were lurking there.

Young Gary put the dirty dishes into the sink, liberally squirting them with washing-up liquid before turning on the hot tap. "Oh, don't say that grandad. Mr Sutton'll be fed up if you don't. He can't afford to run his car there if you don't go. And anyway, after the exams I'll be going. How will I get there if Mr Sutton packs it in."

"We'll see, we'll see. I'll just go and get changed while you finish them dishes. A grand little housemaid, you are. You can come again." George went into his bedroom to get ready.

The click of ball on bat echoed around the empty ground. George huddled in his overcoat, his knarled hands cocooned in woollen gloves. But the sun was shining, and in his head he could hear murmurs of "Well-played", "Good shot", and the occasional ripple of clapping.

"Two overs to go, and ten runs to win. Careful George, don't take any chances."

He strode out to the wicket, asking for middle and leg. The ball arched towards him as he took his swing.

"A six, a six. Good old George!"

He took a deep breath and as the next ball came down he stroked it harmlessly to square leg. The next one was a bouncer and he struck out sending it between square leg and leg-stump, right to the boundary for a four. Cheering, shouting and clapping resounded from every corner.

"Are you alright, grandad? Are you warm enough?" Gary put his hand on his grandad's shoulder.

"Ooh, oh... Yes, yes, champion." George shook himself from his reverie.

"Did you see my innings? Forty-four, the highest score. Not bad eh?" Gary was grinning from ear to ear, full of his own importance.

"I did that. You'll be in the Yorkshire side yet. We'll call in on Fred Sutton on the way back and tell him we'll send off for our membership.

AUTUMN LEAVES

Jean E Owen

Jim was mean. His father had been mean and his grandfather too. It was a family tradition. His body was thin and stretched as if he had been rolled out like pastry to make the most of too little. Bony wrists stuck out from too short sleeves and he could never get trousers long enough.

It was April and cold for Spring but Jim used his heating according to the calendar, not the temperature. He studied pictures of farm machinery in the catalogue he was reading.

"If only I could afford some of this lot. I spend more time mending than using that damned old tractor." Sighing, he turned on the forty watt bulb which dangled over the scrubbed kitchen table. Shivering in the chill, he ate his supper then went to bed. Blankets were the cheapest form of heating he knew.

Jane stretched her slippered feet towards the comforting warmth of the log fire. She smiled as she picked a brochure from the pile she'd collected at the travel agents. Dipping her fingers into a box of coffee creams the smile faded as she paused to listen, then shook her head. "Of course mother isn't calling me. She can't be." Jane settled back to enjoy her evening.

Jane was a few pounds over-weight, it looked more on her small-boned height of five feet. Her glossy hair had begun to show streaks of grey. But she still had a round pink-cheeked face. Two lines were deepening between thick eyebrows caused by not wearing her glasses as often as she should. A log dropped in the fire showering sparks. Jane looked up from the brochure and began smoothing her eyebrows.

"I suppose I'd better go to bed. Got to get my beauty sleep. Prince Charming may be waiting for me at the Harvest dance tomorrow. What a romantic fool I am. Past my sell-by date I am, as mother often reminded me."

Her reflections ended when she heard a "Miaow" at the door. "I'm coming Cleo. I know it's bed time." Jane let the cat in and carried her, purring, to bed.

Jim spent a frustrating day repairing his old tractor. His thoughts returned to money. "I'd even marry a rich woman, if I could find one. Fat chance there is of that round here, but would it be worth it? I don't like women much; always talking."

The village of Hopthorn was spread out which made the community centre an important meeting place. Most people met there often, either in the bar, dance hall or the family room. Gossip was the entertainment. Nothing was secret for long.

Jane looked at herself in the mirror, smoothed the folds of her new dress and tweaked her just-permed hair. She smiled at herself then her hand flew to her mouth. "Whoops, nearly forgot my tooth." She popped the wired tooth into her mouth and grinned widely into the mirror. "That's better. Prince Charming wouldn't fall for a gap tooth smile."

Climbing into her old car, Jane set off for her weekend pleasure, seeing people and having a good gossip.

Jim had his weekly bath, donned his only suit and chose a tie from the four he possessed, brushing the bit of pepper and salt hair on his head. He drove off to his Saturday treat, two pints of beer. If he had more someone else paid. This didn't happen often as he never bought for anybody.

Jim and Jane parked next to each other. "Hello Jim. Hasn't it been a lovely sunny day?"

"Too warm if you'd a tractor to mend like I had."

"Well, you'll enjoy a pint then."

"If they haven't put it up again." Jim grumbled.

They reached the entrance and parted company. Jim to the bar. Jane to the dance.

At midnight the bar closed and the band dispersed. People drifted off calling out goodnight, each mellowed by a pleasant evening.

Jane turned her car key but nothing happened. "Oh, not again. I must have left the interior light on. Now the battery's flat."

Jim heard Jane trying to start her car. "Women! Do I have to help her?" He looked round, but the car park was empty. "Well, I'm not getting out. She'll have to come to me."

"Er, Jim, have you got any jump leads?"

"Not here. They're at home. Leave the car until tomorrow. I'll give you a lift, even though it's out of my way."

Jane got in and as usual when in Jim's company for long, she felt compelled to gabble. "It's very quiet without mother since she died."

"Huh, your mother. She never did approve of me. That's why you're an old maid."

"Well, you didn't like mother and I am lonely without her. Anyway, I thought there were no more surprises left for me, but I got one last week. Now everything's sorted out, mother's left me comfortably off. I'd always thought we were poor."

"So did I. Lucky you. Nobody ever left me anything. Here we are then." Jim stopped and Jane struggled to get down the high Land Rover step. "You ring me in the morning. I'll fetch some jump leads."

The Land Rover moved off. Jane called out "Goodnight and thank you," but Jim didn't speak.

Jane climbed into bed and picked up a holiday brochure. On the cover was a picture of a good looking man and a bikini clad woman. "A cruise, now that would be nice. Perhaps not a bikini though. A swimsuit can look just as good. But dare I go on my own? I'm so used to having mother. I wonder if... Well, it's an idea." Throwing the last of the coffee creams into the bin, Jane picked up the phone.

Jim scraped his fry-up supper onto a plate, just as the phone rang. "Blast the thing. Hello. Oh, Jane. Now what is it? I'm just having my supper. A what? Well, I don't know now. Ring me tomorrow."

Hope Station

Catherine Clark

Muriel pressed the buzzer outside the confused section of the nursing home. Her sister Dolly called it Hope Station because it was somewhere you waited with hope. Through the layers of double glazing she could just make out Dolly's watery figure. Dolly, sat on her throne-like chair taking off and putting on her tights. She was in fine working form that morning, her legs moving in perfect rhythm, perfect time like the pistons of a steam engine.

As Muriel opened the inner door she felt a warm rush of air and caught the sweet smell of urine. She had entered into another world. It was like stepping onto the tarmac of a foreign country.

She picked up a margarine tub from the chair beside her sister, filled with sweet papers and gnarled pieces of chewing gum. She handed the tub over to the Nurse. Shuffling to the edge of the seat she arranged her skirt, so that the buttons faced the same way as she did.

"How's she been this week?"

The Nurse put her hand on Muriel's shoulder.

"Just the same, the same old Dolly. She collects anything, all the bits and pieces the visitors leave behind." Muriel waited for Dolly to finish pulling up her tights. Now she had her attention.

"I went to a Christmas concert last night Dolly."

Dolly picked up a bus ticket that had dropped onto the carpet from Muriel's pocket.

" I went to St. Jude's, you know St. Jude's Dolly, you were married there. The choral society were singing Vivaldi's *Gloria*. It was alright for an amateur concert. But I don't think you'd have liked it Dolly...it wasn't really your thing."

Dolly stared at the lady preparing the tea trolley.

"Hey, where's my beaker juice...you are the beaker people aren't you?"

"It's on its way love."

Dolly groaned, she looked bored and once again started to unpeel her tights. Muriel became irritated by her sister's blatent lack of interest in her visit.

"Shall I tell you what I really thought, sat in St. Jude's Dolly? I really thought that how ridiculous it would be for someone like you, someone stark raving mad, to enjoy Vivaldi. It would be like, well it would be like the Queen cheering on the terraces at Elland Road."

Dolly pointed her big toe into the left stocking and carefully began the process of covering her legs.

"I mean just look at the state of you Dolly, tomato sauce stains on your cardigan, hair all over the place. You used to be so refined. I wish to God you'd stop doing that tight business, it's really getting on my nerves."

Dolly was more interested in a piece of tinsel she had found in the edge of the gusset in her tights. The tea lady arrived with the trolley.

"Cheeky little magpie aren't you Dolly?"

"Magpie" said Dolly "Is that my name Magpie, Dolly, Magpie, Dolly, what is it? It's things like that that stick you know woman, just like that nice hard wrinkly bit of chewing gum I found underneath the table at visiting time."

The nurse gave Dolly a beaker and Muriel a cup and saucer. Muriel hated the beakers.

The tea lady was fascinated by Dolly doing her tights.

"Do you know, Roy Castle really ought to see you doing that love, he'd be amazed by your dedication."

"Well he can't" said Dolly.

"Of course he can, we'd be on Record Breakers. Don't you want to be on the telly Dolly?"

"He's dead, he's dead, he's dead," snapped Dolly. "Do you think he'll give me a record now, how many times, are you a deaf person?"

Muriel felt completely rejected. Dolly was getting all the attention. But then again she always did. She always had the boyfriends when they were younger. Muriel used to mop up the ones that Dolly had ditched, like discarded crumbs of despair. They were like putty in her hands. Even now she was on the outside of the conversation and Dolly was supposed to be the outsider, the one shut away from the world. It just wasn't fair.

"In the interval Dolly, I was looking around the church hall. And do you know there were lots of middle-aged women, just like me in their hushpuppies, furlined boots and tweed coats. But do you know in the middle section there was this dead georgeous chap wearing patent chestnut brogues and a trench coat."

Dolly looked intently at Muriel and sucked noisily on her beaker.

"You'd have liked him Dolly. Anyway, I watched him unfasten his trench coat and stretch his arm seductively along the bench behind this woman in a red cape and a black lacquered buffant." Muriel started to cry.

"If you weren't mad, if you weren't mad Dolly you'd have been sat there in that middle section, but I would still have been stuck with the fur lined boots brigade. But he did look exciting Dolly. Oh God, why can't I have an exciting boyfriend?"

Muriel wiped her eyes with her sleeve, took off her coat and relaxed back into the chair.

"It was really funny though Dolly, there was this woman sat at the front of the church. She had this hat on, it looked just like a hot cross bun. I desperately wanted to ask her why she was wearing a hot cross bun at a Christmas concert. But I couldn't, I wanted to but I just couldn't. You could have asked her Dolly and everyone would just smile and gently remove you from the building."

Muriel missed Dolly. It was as if she had found a new life, with new friends and now they had nothing to say to each other. But Dolly could have a future, she could sit in an art gallery taking off and putting on her tights. People would comment on how the browness of the American tan contrasted with the bluey whiteness of her legs. 'Why not?' thought Muriel, people trek all the way up the Himalayas to see the Dali Lama, why not catch a bus to see their Dolly at the city gallery? One thing was clear, Dolly had a future and Muriel was going home to watch the Generation Game on the telly.

SILKS

Tracey Knaggs

It was with some trepidation that she pressed the intercom button to the flat. A loud voice boomed out at her,

"Is that you Shauna?"

"Yes," came the timid response.

"Well what are you waiting for, get your ass up here girl!"

She entered the apartment. The voice shouted from the bedroom,

"Pour yourself a drink, hurry up. I've had three gins already."

Shauna was just about to replace the cap when Dolores took over.

"I'll show you. Give it here."

There was scarcely room for tonic water.

"My God! What have you got on? You look like my Gran. I'll lend you my new short black dress, come on. And hurry up with that drink."

"I'm not sure it's my style?"

"Because you haven't got one girl. It's fine. Come on. Let's give 'em hell."

The pub was packed with talent hunters. Dolores' eyes sparkled as she elbowed her way to the bar.

"I'll order, you can pay."

Shauna fumbled for her purse. Dolores struck up a conversation with some guy and allowed him to buy their drinks.

"You can't let him get me one as well! It's you he's talking to."

"Oh shut up. I don't believe in equal opportunities."

The gin began to take effect. Shauna had not felt this free for years. Her confidence blossomed.

After a few more drinks Dolores grabbed Shauna's arm.

"Come on. Let's go to the loo."

She dragged her out of the pub.

"What a drip. Quick, let's go to Silks."

"Without saying goodnight ? Don't you feel guilty?"

"What for?"

The dance beat thudded through Shauna's body. She was anxious as she looked down the queue.

"What's wrong?"

"I'll be so embarrassed if that man sees us."

"Stop worrying. Christ, he's had the pleasure of our company for the past hour. That's a fantastic deal!"

Shauna laughed. She'd known Dolores for years through work but never socially. She'd often envied her confidence and glamour. Now she would have to add brass-faced cheek to the list. She saw a reflection of herself in a shop window.

"God, is that me? My husband would have a fit if he could see me in these clothes."

"Bugger him. He's away with his friends having a good time. But I bet we can have more fun tonight than he'll manage all weekend."

This conversation was overheard by two men. They eagerly offered to pay the girl's entrance fee.

"Thank you. You're real gents. Aren't they Shauna?"

"I'm confused Dolores. Men have never offered to pay for things for me before."

"Well there's no wonder in the gear you were coming out in is there girl! Come on, we're off in and I need the loo."

"Oh, you're not going to pull that stunt again are you?"

"What, before I've allowed them to buy me some drinks? Get real. Now you go with them and watch that tart in red. Don't let her take my man."

Shauna felt lost as she was led to a table. One man sat close to her while the other went to the bar. She tried to pull the short dress down. The man stopped her.

"Really, it's fine. My name's Jon by the way."

Her tongue leapt into action.

"I'm Shauna. I don't wear clothes like this normally, or drink much, or come to these type of places because I'm happily married and I..."

"Stop. It's OK. I can see that by the way you act. You're not like your friend are you?"

She looked at his face and was drawn deep into his eyes. She knew she could trust him.

The other man returned with a tray of drinks and Dolores clinging to his arm. She lent across the table and shouted down Shauna's ear.

"And where were you? There I was struggling with my body suit and the party poppers on the gusset, by the time I left the loo that cow in red was making a move. But don't worry I've sorted her out."

Dolores smiled at her man and they were soon kissing. Shauna was glad when Jon asked her to dance. The DJ played Oasis, Pulp and Blur, music she adored and her husband detested. She was in her element.

"I love to dance, but my husband won't."

"Then I think he's a fool."

It didn't seem two minutes before the slow music started. Shauna pulled away as Jon moved closer. She hadn't anticipated the night would be like this. The look in his eyes. There was something different about him. She couldn't help it. The pit of her stomach rose inside her as the look became a passionate kiss.

It wasn't long before Dolores tapped Shauna on the shoulder.

"I'm taking my party poppers to Dave's. See you later."

Shauna didn't have time to react. Dolores had gone. The nightclub no longer felt like a safe haven for pleasure, and Shauna was uneasy. Jon took hold of her hands.

"Don't worry, I'll see you get home. Come on. I'll call a taxi."

There was a huge queue at the taxi rank and the cool night air began to make them shiver.

"Why don't you go Jon? I'll be OK."

"If it's not too far I could walk you home."

She eagerly held out her hand and began to lead the way. They seemed to reach the doorstep too soon. She put the key into the lock. Her heart was racing as she turned to bid Jon goodnight. He was already edging away. He smiled and their eyes met again. She could feel herself lurching forwards in desperation. He couldn't leave without giving her a final kiss. She knew it was wrong but his eyes seemed to control her now.

"Thank you for walking me home. Suppose this is where you kiss me goodnight."

He climbed onto the step and stroked her face. She could smell his aftershave as she gently kissed his fingers. The look came again. She felt weak as he turned the key and opened the door. He led her inside. She followed in silence locking the door behind them.

The Magic Scarf

Mary Maxwell

Why had Gran stopped reading? Just at an exciting part, thought Hannah. She picked up the book that had dropped to the floor and screwed up Gran's old silk scarf she used as a comforter.

"Look Gran, I can do magic" she said , packing the scarf into her tiny palm, then releasing it to billow out like an inflated balloon. Gran didn't answer, she'd nodded off. Perhaps she'd like to hold the scarf. As Hannah tucked it into her hand, Gran's fingers caressed the soft silk and her face wrinkled into a smile like screwed up tissue paper.

She was happy. She was 18 again unwrapping her presents and just as the scarf had sprung from Hannah's hand, so it did again from the confines of the wrapping paper. She tucked the gaily coloured silk into her belt where it floated as she glided to a waltz, fluttered to an energetic polka and protected her shoulders from the cool evening air, as she walked in the garden later.

"Ssshhh, Gran's asleep" said Hannah as Margaret, her mother entered the room. "She's smiling. Perhaps she's having a nice dream."

Gran moved the silk scarf through her fingers, just as she had as a child when her night light cast shadows on the ceiling and she couldn't sleep.

It was now her Whitsuntide dress and mum was arranging the flowers on her new straw bonnet.

"Mind you don't catch the threads of your dress when

you get up to recite your poem" she was saying. Mum had spent hours smocking and embroidering. She was proud of her work.

The soft silk now became Gran's evening dress. Worn at her first Minden ball. Contrasting with the rough feel of the uniform worn by her partner guiding her gently around the floor. His eyes reflecting the blue of her dress, looking into her's saying "I love you" as he slipped the sparkling ring on her finger. His habit of raising one eyebrow, giving the impression of a lopsided smile as he traced the outline of her nose with his finger.

"Can I have it back now Gran?"

Her doze was interrupted by Hannah trying to release the comforter from Gran's arthritic fingers, but she wouldn't yield. She must hang on. Just as she'd hung on to her children when she'd carried them to the font in their christening gown. The silk had a special smell then. Cherished silk. Used only at christenings then laid away again in an old tin trunk and scattered with sachets of lavender and pot pourri. She rubbed the scarf between finger and thumb as though the life in her body would fade away like the colours of the scarf if she let go.

Colourless silk. The creamy white silk of her wedding gown. Being escorted down the aisle on the arm of her father. Sad at losing her and squeezing her hand in a reassuring gesture. To Richard, looking immaculate in dress uniform and ceremonial sash. The discarding of her wedding gown before being whisked away on honeymoon. The unpacking of her trousseau. Packed by her mother who'd held the soft silk to her cheek and wept nostalgic tears.

Hold on. Hold on.

She was holding the ribbon of the Maypole with hot sticky hands in the warm May sunshine. Little bodies skipping, bobbing and weaving to the music. Miss Jones thumping out the rhythm with her foot and grinning from ear to ear encouraging the children to smile.

The dream faded as Hannah's distant voice scolded her doll. A strong bond existed between Hannah and Gran. So much like herself in younger days. Some dark brown hair neatly cut in a fringe, surrounding a chubby rounded face. Her habit of screwing up her nose when she was displeased, Gran sometimes felt she was living her life again through Hannah. She could almost anticipate her every thought.

"You naughty doll you've spilled your milk" she was saying.

"Now say your prayers and get into bed. You're making Gran sad."

Prayers - the prayer book with the silk cross stained with salty tears. Marking the page of the hymn for those in peril on the sea. Tears shed for a brother she'd loved and fought, buried in a wet salty tomb on the ocean bed. Her mother in a black silk blouse, trying to hide her grief to keep the rest of the family strong, but betrayed by dark brown unsmiling eyes and trembling fingers.

"Your legs feel cold Gran" said Hannah, taking the silk scarf and placing it over her knees.

Gran was now clad in her first pair of pure silk stockings. Fully fashioned and luxurious. Rolled on with great care. Making sure the dark seams at the back kept perfectly straight. The horror of having them handed back laddered after her sister borrowed them for a date.

"I wish Gran would finish my story" said Hannah.

"Later dear, she needs her afternoon nap" mum replied.

Gran was irritated by the vague mumblings. She hated being disturbed. Pulling the scarf from her knees she draped the smooth silk over her eyes and settled back into a comfortable doze.

She was now sitting at the top table, the silk scarf draped around her frail shoulders. The Golden Wedding cake waiting to be cut. The sedate old man at her side with his twinkling blue eyes looking into hers, cupping her face with his hands, kissing the tip of her turned up nose saying with pride,

"Well we made it old girl. Shall we dance."

They took to the floor to the strains of the Anniversary Waltz. The years fell away. He was the sure footed young man with the raised eyebrow and quirky smile.

She felt heady in his presence.

"Hold me Richard" she whispered.

She awoke as the scarf fell to the floor. The dream faded, but the magic lived on through Hannah who picked it up, tucked it into her tiny palm and made it disappear.

WORD PICKER

Jean Aldersea

The Word Picker leapt over the television and sat in the waste paper bin.

"Come out of there," said Jean.

"Who me? Who in the world am I? Ah, that's a great puzzle."

"Shut up Word Picker and stop quoting *Alice*. My Wonderland needs a story of one thousand and one words."

The Word Picker wiggled his enormous ears and lifted his head over the edge of the waste paper bin. He was eager to please and bloated with knowledge. "What's the problem, woman?"

Jean felt most inadequate as she confessed, "I have searched in the Dictionary and found millions of words, all floppy and unattached. Could you please help me join them together?"

Word Picker looked Jean straight in the eyes. "Read some good books, study them carefully and learn to write like an expert."

"But, I can't write anything which makes sense."

"Edit, edit, cut out the waffle. Follow me and use your imagination. There was a little blackbird pecked off her nose."

"Whose nose?"

"Your's of course."

The Word Picker rushed out of the room and down the garden path. Jean, determined to keep sight of him, grabbed her distance glasses. 'Why the tool shed?' she thought. It was then she noticed the blackbird's nest up in the rafters. It looked quite ordinary, just like last year's and the year's before. She began to recite.

High on a ledge a blackbird's nest,
she took no rest, until well lined and warm,
a home for her eggs began to form.

Once the nest was safely made
five speckled eggs the blackbird laid
I opened the door, she did not move
fear overcome by inborn love.

She sat so still and silently peeped out at me.

"Blackbird, if only I could trust myself to life unseen, like you. High on your ledge, lovingly believing whatever will be, will be."

The blackbird stared over the rim of the nest. "What a load of rubbish. Next door's cat ate most of last year's fledgelings." Then she screamed to her twittering family, "Off with her nose, off with her nose."

Next door's cat was standing in the flower bed. 'What a daft place to sell newspapers', thought Jean as she stepped carefully over the rose bushes to get a closer look at the placard round his neck.

The Word Picker ripped out the front page of the newspaper and stuffed it into Jean's hand. "Read all about it, read all about it."

Jean read the headlines and shuddered. 'WORLD EPIDEMIC OF WRITER'S CRAMP'. Word Picker yelled at the cat, "Go sell your newspapers elsewhere."

"Come on Jean, never mind the headlines. Edit, edit, cut out the waffle and follow me through the Library to Letterland. I want you to meet my nephew, Waffle."

The Word Picker scurried along the avenue of bookcases until he reached a large volume of *War and Peace*. Sliding it aside he revealed a small door on which hung a sign, *Silence, Reading Room*. Word Picker grabbed hold of Jean and, lifting her above the top shelves, he dropped her over the threshold.

"Meet my nephew Waffle. He spends most of the time wasting words." Word Picker nodded toward a table full of newspapers. Jean was surprised to see next door's cat tripping over his placard as he raced frantically round the Reading Room, screaming, "Read all about it!" Behind him fluttered Blackbird twittering, "Scandalous, scandalous, peck off her nose." Waffle clasped a newspaper in grubby fingers, his unruly red hair escaping from under a crumpled Mortarboard. Jean smiled and held out her hand. "Pleased to meet you Mr Waffle."

Waffle glared. "Bunkum! You have started a war of words. Just look at the state of those two. I'll see you in court this afternoon. Better have a good story, or else!"

Word Picker yelled, "Jean, get out of the Library. Follow me. We must not be late for your trial."

"My trial?" Jean gasped. "What am I accused of?"

Wordpicker grinned. "Writing a rhyme without reason; stealing words; and breaking and entering into a fairy story."

As they reached the Court Room door Word Picker whispered, "Diplomacy, conformity and mind your Ps and Qs."

The Judge read the charges. "Breaking and entering into a fairy story containing one thousand and one words; writing a rhyme without reason; and stealing newspaper headlines." The Judge spoke to Word Picker. "Can you explain your client's actions?"

"Yes, My Lord. She told me life is too sour to be consumed without a sugar coating." Word Picker sat down beside Jean. "Let me do the talking, woman. Your vocabulary is rudimental and recognisably rustic."

Jean understood the simple message: "Shut up!"

Blackbird hopped into the Witness box and pulled the poem from under her wing. "That woman twittered away and wrote a poem, a complete misrepresentation of my family life. She read it out loud, so I shall sue for slander."

Next door's cat leaped into the Witness box. He held up a newspaper. "She has torn my paper and stolen the words to use in a story, exactly one thousand and one words, to make up the plot."

Waffle slipped into the box and waffled on and on about how Jean and her wicked ways had started a war of words. Everyone in the Court room fell asleep.

Jean and the Word Picker made a quick exit and caught the last bus home.

Next door's cat yelled, "Read all about it!" and waved a new placard 'MYSTERY WRITER DISAPPEARS'.

Word Picker was very tired as he ran up the garden path and climbed over a pile of pens and a mountain of used scrap paper. It had all been worthwhile. The story was completed.

Jean put the kettle on and made a cup of tea. Time to write another story. She reached for a clean sheet of paper, only to hear a voice from the waste bin. "Edit, edit, cut out the waffle."

THE WAY BACK

Jean Mengham

"Drink up, Dad." Dan rose to his feet and picked up his empty glass. George drained the last of his beer and set the glass down. The convivial sounds of the pub soothed him and he smiled to himself, the anger of yesterday all but forgotten. He'd been wrong, he knew, but when Dan had told him that he had a place at Oxford his first reaction had been a scathing "Oxford! Why there? Agricultural College would make more sense."

Dan had turned on him viciously, shouting "What makes you think I want to be a farmer. You've assumed too much!" Things had been said that should have remained unspoken and Dan had slammed out of the room. The next morning he had gone. "He wanted you to be proud of him. Now see what you've done you stubborn old fool." Mary had been bitter.

Dan manoeuvred his way back to their table with two brimming glasses and set them down with care. George looked at his son with pride and pleasure. Tall, broad-shouldered, his blonde hair shining in the light. A strong jaw but a kind and gentle mouth. No wonder the girls were all after him!

"Why haven't we done this before, Dad?" Dan leaned towards him. "Talked I mean."

"Your grandfather never talked much. Well, not to me, not even to your grandmother come to think of it. Perhaps it's a family gene. He was a miserable old bugger," mused George. "It didn't matter how much you did he didn't seem to care - except once." He was silent for a moment remembering the wizened, cancer-ridden body. His father had laid a claw of a hand on his arm and he'd leaned over to him to hear the words "I'm proud of you, son". They were the last words he'd spoken.

"Approved of your Mother, though."

"How did you two meet?" asked Dan.

George chuckled. "At the local hop. We had proper dances in those days, not this jigging about you do nowadays. Best looking lass there." He could see her in his mind's eye still, in her blue dress, the colour of her eyes and her corn gold hair falling over her shoulders. "God knows what she saw in me. Wouldn't have asked her out, but my pals egged me on. I was proper flummoxed when she said 'Yes'."

Dan laughed. "Then you plucked up courage to ask her to marry you."

"Well, not exactly." George confessed. "We went out for quite a while and then one night, blow me if she didn't ask me when we were getting wed."

"You'd probably be courting her still if she hadn't." Dan teased.

"More than likely," his father conceded.

"So it was 'happy ever after'." Dan leaned back and took a sip of his beer.

George was silent for a moment. "Not exactly. Our Sarah wasn't our first bairn. It was a bad time, Dan. Your mother took it very hard." Even now he could still feel the pain. He'd been certain it would be a boy and it was, who'd lived only two hours. As he'd held the small body in his arms and looked down at the tiny waxen face stamped with his features he had bent his head and wept, ashamed of his weakness. Mary had withdrawn into a place where he could not reach her and all the happiness and gaiety had left. He had gathered his pain into himself and thrown himself into work, the only way he knew of coping.

"It must have been difficult when Sarah was on the way. I mean, worrying about things turning out OK."

"It was." George smiled thinking of Sarah. After her birth it was as though life had flowed back into their marriage. "Then you came along and made the family complete." George said. They'd named him after George's grandfather and he'd said, "Another Farmer Dan."

The landlord called time and they went out into the cold night. "Let's walk up to the top pasture." Dan suggested.

George nodded and shrugged his overcoat on.

The moon was full and the fields were bathed in its soft light. They walked in silence each with his own thoughts.

Until yesterday Dan hadn't realized how much the farm meant to his father. He had been so proud of his place at Oxford but his father had taken all the joy of his achievement. The assumption that he would work on the farm - that more education was unnecessary - had infuriated him and he'd slammed the door on his father and next morning left the house, for good, he'd thought. Thank goodness he'd had the sense to return.

They reached the top and leaned their arms on the five-barred gate. George thought back to the figure waving to him that morning. He had been unloading the hay from the tractor. The clouds had lifted and the sun was warm on his back promising spring at last. The gulls had wheeled about his head rising and falling like scraps of paper in a gale, their harsh cries drowning the lowing of the herd. He had not needed to hear the cry of "Dad" to know that Dan had returned and he was to be given a second chance.

He felt like an old ship that had survived a huge storm and had reached a peaceful harbour at last.

"I'm sorry, Dad." Dan turned his head towards his father.

"It's me that should be sorry, Dan."

"I wanted you to be proud of me."

"I am, right proud. Whatever you do I'll still love you." There, he'd said it, thought George, and meant it.

He turned towards the farm nestling in the hollow of the hills. "Best get back, your mother'll be wondering what's happened to us." Together the two men strode down the hill.

"I want to be a vet. I know it's a long haul but it's what I want to do."

George nodded. "First vet in the family, eh. That'll really be something."